DISNEY'S

THE LITTLE MERMAID

ARIEL THE SPY

DISNEY'S
THE LITTLE
MERMAID

ARIEL THE SPY

by M. J. Carr

illustrations by Fred Marvin

DISNEY
PRESS

NEW YORK

Library of Congress Catalog Card Number: 92-54512

ISBN 1-56282-372-8

FIRST EDITION

1 3 5 7 9 10 8 6 4 2

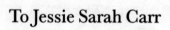

To Jessie Sarah Carr

Look for these other books in the series:

ARISTA'S NEW BOYFRIEND
GREEN-EYED PEARL
NEFAZIA VISITS THE PALACE
REFLECTIONS OF ARSULU
THE SAME OLD SONG

DISNEY'S

THE LITTLE MERMAID

ARIEL THE SPY

BRRRIINNNGG! The alarm clock went off. In King Triton's undersea palace it was a typical Monday morning. The King's seven daughters—Aquata, Andrina, Arista, Attina, Adella, Alana, and Ariel—all woke up at the same time to get ready for school. That meant that seven mermaids were scrambling about, getting in each other's way, hunting for their hairbrushes, and vying for the mirror in the royal dressing room. In other words, it meant chaos.

"Adella!" complained Aquata. "The rest of us have to use the mirror, too!"

"Why are you wasting your breath?" Attina asked Aquata. "Adella *always* monopolizes the mirror."

"Yes," said Aquata, "but today she's taking even longer than usual."

Adella did not take her eyes from the mirror. "I'm giving myself a beauty treatment," she said. "And I'll thank you to leave me in peace while I do it."

Aquata shook her head in exasperation. She looked around at her other sisters. They were all ready to leave, all of them, that is, with one exception. Her youngest sister, Ariel, was curled up in a corner, engrossed in a book.

"Ariel," Arista called from the doorway, "are you coming?"

Ariel didn't answer.

"I *said*," Arista repeated, much louder this time, "ARIEL, ARE YOU COMING?"

"Hmm? What?" Ariel asked distractedly.

"Uh-oh," Andrina joined in, laughing. "It looks as if Ariel's got book fever."

Attina, who loved books more than

anything, swam over to Ariel. "What are you reading?" she asked eagerly.

"It's a book about Mata Herring," said Ariel.

"Mata Herring?" said Alana. "Wasn't she the woman who set the record for speed swimming?"

"No," said Ariel. "Mata Herring was a famous spy, and she got involved in all sorts of intrigue."

"Really?" said Attina. She leaned closer to Ariel, but the other sisters turned away. "Come on," they said. "We don't have time for book fever. We've got to get to school." And off they went, leaving Attina and Ariel with their heads in the book.

"Look at this picture," Ariel said to Attina. She pointed to a photo of Mata Herring wearing an exotic disguise with flowing veils and strings of pearls. She was standing next to an enemy general who sported a big mustache. "I'm reading the book for a school project," Ariel explained. "Mr. Chubb has asked us all to do reports on famous women in history."

"Oh!" laughed Attina. "Mr. Chubb! I

should have known that your favorite teacher was responsible for this."

"Let's go!" someone said.

The sisters looked up to see Coral, one of Ariel's classmates, standing in the doorway. "We're going to be late!" she said.

As the three mermaids hurried toward school, Ariel sighed and said, "I can't wait to see Mr. Chubb!"

"Me, neither," said Coral. "He's my favorite teacher in the whole ocean! Do you think he's going to win the Teacher of the Year award this year?"

"This is definitely the year," said Ariel. "It's got to be! This famous women in history project is the best school assignment I've ever had. I can't wait to tell Mr. Chubb how much fun I'm having reading the book!"

When the mermaids got to school, Ariel and Coral swam quickly up to their classroom. Ariel was hoping to talk to Mr. Chubb before school started. But when she swam into the classroom, Mr. Chubb wasn't there. Instead, there was a merman she didn't know sitting at Mr. Chubb's desk. The bell rang and the merman introduced himself. "Hello," he said. "My name is Mr. Kipper. I'm afraid Mr. Chubb has been called away unexpectedly, so I'm taking his place."

Ariel's hand shot up. "When is Mr. Chubb coming back?" she asked.

"I'm hoping he'll return by tomorrow," said Mr. Kipper.

"But where has he gone?" asked Ariel.

Mr. Kipper's brow furrowed, and he stared fixedly out the window as if deep in thought.

"Mr. Chubb's gone to warmer waters," he said finally. Then he turned back to the class and said, "Open your math books to page forty-eight. Pronto," he added with a wink.

Ariel looked up, surprised. *Pronto!* That's what Mr. Chubb always said! And how did Mr. Kipper know that the class was indeed on page forty-eight of the math book? Ariel looked around the class. Mr. Kipper hadn't seemed to want to talk about Mr. Chubb. Ariel found that to be a little strange, but no one else seemed to think anything was wrong. They were all opening their math books to page forty-eight.

Ariel didn't feel much like studying, though—not if Mr. Chubb wasn't there. She hid her Mata Herring book inside her math book and opened that instead. It fell open to the photograph of Mata Herring and the enemy general. Ariel put her finger over the general's mustache. Without the mustache, she thought, the general looked kind of like Mr. Kipper.

"Pssst!" Ariel angled the book toward Coral and passed her friend a note that read, "Do you think this looks like Mr. Kipper?"

Coral giggled. She passed a note back. "A little," it read.

At the front of the classroom, Mr. Kipper was droning on, giving some sort of lecture about some sort of complex mathematical computations.

But Ariel didn't pay any attention to him until she heard Mr. Kipper say, "Now put your books away and take out a clean sheet of paper and a pencil. We're going to have a little test on the material I just explained."

Test! Ariel waved her hand frantically until Mr. Kipper called on her. Maybe he

just didn't understand how things were done in this classroom. Maybe if she just explained. . . .

"Mr. Chubb never gives surprise tests," she said in her most authoritative voice. "In fact, he hardly gives any tests at all. Mostly he just assigns homework and projects."

Mr. Kipper raised his eyebrows skeptically. "A clean sheet of paper and a pencil," he repeated. "We'll need to know exactly what this class has learned today and what it hasn't."

Ariel winced and took out a clean sheet of paper. She was done-for now. But what did Mr. Kipper mean when he said that "we" would need to know what the class has learned? Who was "we"?

As she bent to shut her Mata Herring book, Ariel glanced again at the photo inside. Mr. Kipper was somehow looking more and more like the enemy general, she thought—nasty, sinister, and not to be trusted at all.

2

The next morning, Ariel was out of bed and rubbing the sleep out of her eyes before the alarm went off. Mr. Kipper had said that Mr. Chubb would be gone only one day, and Ariel wanted to get to school early to welcome him back.

She swam to the window to see if Coral was coming, but there was no sign of her friend. Ariel flipped her hair impatiently. "I *told* Coral to meet me early today," she said out loud to herself.

Ariel swam outside to wait for Coral in front of the palace. To pass the time, she opened her Mata Herring book and read the chapter about Herring and the general. Wow! Ariel thought as she flipped through the pages. The evil general, it turned out, had suddenly appeared one day to replace another general who had mysteriously been called away. Mata Herring had been the first to suspect that this new general was not exactly what he seemed.

"Hey there!" came a voice. Coral was rounding the corner. "Am I late?" she asked.

"I'll say," Ariel said. "Let's go!"

As the two friends swam off to school, Ariel chattered on to her friend about mysterious disappearances and enemy spies and Mata Herring's bravery. "I can't wait to tell Mr. Chubb how *fascinating* this all is," she gushed.

But again, when Ariel swam into the classroom, Mr. Chubb wasn't there. Mr. Kipper was behind the desk, going through some papers. Ariel and Coral swam up behind him.

"Mr. Kipper," said Coral.

"Oh!" Mr. Kipper jumped when he heard his name. He folded the papers quickly and tucked them into an envelope. The envelope had writing on it, but Ariel couldn't see what it said.

"You startled me," he said. "You two are awfully early for class today."

"We came to talk to Mr. Chubb," said Ariel.

"I'm afraid he won't be here again today," said Mr. Kipper.

"But where is he?" asked Coral.

"He's . . ." Mr. Kipper seemed unsure of what to say. "He'll be up north rather indefinitely, I'm afraid."

"Up north," said Ariel, alert to every word. "Yesterday you said he'd gone to *warmer* waters."

"Did I?" said Mr. Kipper. He didn't say anything more.

"Well, why is Mr. Chubb away?" Ariel persisted. "Is something the matter?"

Mr. Kipper slipped the envelope with the papers into his briefcase. "Mr. Chubb is tied up," he said. "I'm afraid that's all I can say."

Ariel threw Coral a worried glance.

11

"Now, if you don't mind," Mr. Kipper continued, "I'll have to ask you to wait outside a while longer. There are still a few minutes until class, and I have some lessons to prepare."

Ariel and Coral swam out of the classroom. "Didn't you think Mr. Kipper was acting strangely?" Ariel asked Coral. She could barely keep still. "The way he was so startled to see us?"

"Hmm. I didn't notice anything," said Coral.

"The way he was rifling through those papers," Ariel went on. "Why did he get confused about where Mr. Chubb had gone? And why did he say Mr. Chubb was 'tied up'? Didn't you think that was odd that he wouldn't tell us what was going on, and then he used the words *tied up*?"

"It's just an expression," said Coral.

"I know that," said Ariel, "but it sounds kind of sinister."

Coral looked at her friend, unconvinced. "Maybe Mata Herring should be on this case," she said, teasing.

"Maybe," Ariel replied. But *she* was serious.

By this time, the other classmates had arrived, and Mr. Kipper opened the door and started the class by telling everyone to put away their textbooks. "We're going to do things a little differently today," he said.

Then Mr. Kipper passed out materials he had typed up himself. Ariel looked at the handout. There were too many numbers on the page. Ariel thought it looked as if it had been specifically designed to confuse them all.

Mr. Kipper swam up and down the rows, making sure everyone received a handout. When Mr. Kipper passed Ariel's desk, Ariel noticed the envelope edging out of his pocket. She saw what was written on it: "Teacher of the Year Contest"!

Ariel fidgeted at her desk, waiting for the morning to be over. When the lunch bell rang, she streaked over to Coral's desk. "There's something I've got to talk to you about," she whispered. "Come on!"

"What is it?" Coral asked when the two mermaids reached the hallway.

"Shhh," said Ariel. She nodded toward Mr. Kipper, who was swimming past them, headed for the teachers lounge. Ariel noticed that he was carrying Mr. Chubb's briefcase! She waited until he passed.

But before Ariel could point the briefcase out to Coral, Adella swam up. "Hey," she said, glancing back over her shoulder at Mr. Kipper. "Who's that cute guy?"

"That's no cute guy," said Ariel. "That's our teacher! And there's something suspicious about him!"

"Suspicious?" said Coral. "Oh, Ariel. You don't still think that, do you?"

"Yesterday he practically said he was going to give our test scores to some kind of group. Who knows what evil things they'll do with them!"

"What *group*? And what in the world can be *evil* about test scores?" asked Coral. "Ariel, what are you talking about?"

"*We*," Ariel insisted. "He said *we* need to know exactly what the class knows."

"That's just a way of speaking."

"But today he handed out a lesson that's too confusing for even a genius to understand!"

"He does things differently from Mr.

Chubb is all," said Coral. "It'll probably take some time for us to get used to him and his ways."

"Coral," Ariel said seriously, "that envelope he had in his pocket—do you know what was printed on it?"

"What?"

" 'Teacher of the Year Contest'!"

"Really?" cried Coral. Now she looked alarmed.

"Here," Ariel said, opening her Mata Herring book. "Look at this picture. Mr. Kipper really does have the same sinister look as the enemy general, doesn't he? Without the mustache, I mean."

Adella laughed out loud. "You think your teacher looks *vaguely* like some villain in a *history* book? Ariel, you *have* had your nose in that book too long. This Mr. Kipper of yours is just a substitute teacher." She smiled and added, "Though he *is* a little cuter than most."

Adella swam off, leaving Ariel and Coral huddled around Ariel's book. Coral stared hard at the photo and shook her head.

"All I know is that it *is* a little weird that

Mr. Kipper has an envelope that says 'Teacher of the Year Contest,'" said Coral.

Finally, thought Ariel, Coral was beginning to see her point.

"So what do you think he's up to?" Coral asked.

"I don't know," said Ariel. "But something just doesn't sit right with me. I knew there was something wrong the first time I laid eyes on him."

"But what can you do about it?" asked Coral.

"Well, I'm not going to lunch," Ariel said determinedly. "I'm going to talk to Ms. Finn! Come on!"

Ms. Finn was the school principal. She wore her silver-gray hair swept up into a loose, poofy topknot, although her hair never seemed to stay up. Wisps of it fell in front of her eyes and uncurled at the nape of her neck.

As Ariel and Coral swam into her office, Ms. Finn looked up from her desk, which was in as much disarray as her hair. When she got up to greet the two young mermaids, she knocked over a pile of books. "Oh my," she said as she reached down to pick them up.

"Ms. Finn . . . ," Ariel began.

"Yes, dears, what can I do for you?" Ms. Finn asked brightly. She scooped up the books and dropped them in a messy pile on her desk.

"It's about Mr. Kipper," said Ariel.

"Mr. Kipper . . . Mr. Kipper . . . ," said Ms. Finn.

"You know," Coral piped in. "Our substitute teacher?"

"Oh yes, of course, of course," said Ms. Finn. "Your substitute teacher. And a lovely man he is, isn't he? We're very lucky to have him on such short notice."

"Actually, I'm a little concerned about him," said Ariel.

"Concerned!" Ms. Finn cut in, alarmed. "Why? Is the poor man ill?"

"I don't think so," said Ariel. "What I mean is, I'm concerned for our class. And for Mr. Chubb."

"And why is that?" asked Ms. Finn. She tucked a stray strand of hair back into her topknot and patted it down.

Ariel looked at Coral for reassurance before she went on. But Coral looked scared.

"Maybe this is silly," Coral whispered to her. "Maybe we ought to just leave now and forget the whole thing."

Ariel closed her eyes to summon up her courage. What would Mata Herring do in a situation like this? she thought. Ariel knew what Mata Herring would do. She'd report whatever information she had. Ariel knew what she must do, too.

"I don't trust Mr. Kipper," she said bluntly.

"Don't trust him?" asked Ms. Finn.

"There's something suspicious about him," said Ariel. "Something very suspicious, actually." She unfolded a list she had tucked into the back of her book.

"You wrote it all down?" asked Coral in surprise.

"I certainly did," said Ariel. "First of all," she said, addressing Ms. Finn, "I saw Mr. Kipper carrying Mr. Chubb's briefcase. Not only that, he's used expressions that only Mr. Chubb uses, as if he's trying to *be* Mr. Chubb. Somehow, when he came into the class, he knew exactly what we were supposed to be doing. He even knew what *page* we were on in our math book. But every time I ask him where Mr. Chubb has gone, he changes his story."

Ariel caught her breath and barreled on.

"Yesterday," she said, "he decided to test us. And he said he was going to tell some other people what our class knows and what it doesn't. Then today he deliberately tried to confuse us. He passed out material that only a genius could read. I, for one, couldn't understand a word of it!"

As Ariel rattled on, Ms. Finn listened politely. Ariel read through her entire list before Ms. Finn spoke.

"Oh, Ariel," she said. "I don't mean to hurt your feelings, but you really don't have a case against your teacher. I'm afraid that what you *do* have is a very vivid imagination, one of the most vivid in the entire school, I suspect. It's a wonderful quality, really. An imagination is a wonderful thing."

"But this isn't my imagination," Ariel protested. "This is serious."

"Ariel," Ms. Finn said firmly, "Mr. Kipper is a fine, upstanding teacher. He comes to

us with impeccable credentials. In fact, I believe he's even been nominated for the Teacher of the Year award. As for Mr. Chubb," she went on, "he sent me a note informing me that he needed to be away, and he suggested Mr. Kipper as his temporary replacement. Now let's see, where did I put that note?" She rooted through the papers on her desk.

"A note!" cried Ariel. "This could be important evidence!"

Ms. Finn pulled a worn, creased note out from under one of her tottering piles. The note read: "Have been called away unexpectedly. Mr. Kipper prepared to take over class."

"Now girls," said Ms. Finn, "surely your time could be put to better use. Story writing or *something* else that would put these extremely vivid imaginations of yours to good work."

With that, Ms. Finn dismissed Ariel and Coral.

"Did you see that note?" Ariel asked Coral when they got outside.

"What about it?" asked Coral.

"What *about* it?" said Ariel. "It was written in a *very* shaky hand. I know Mr. Chubb's handwriting. It's much stronger than that. That note was written by someone who was very upset about something."

"Well, if Mr. Chubb had to go away because of an emergency, of course he'd be upset," said Coral.

"Yes, but did you hear Ms. Finn say that Mr. Kipper's been nominated for Teacher of the Year?"

"He doesn't seem like that great a teacher to me," Coral said, shrugging.

"Exactly!" said Ariel. "He must *know* he wouldn't stand a chance against Mr. Chubb!"

The two mermaids fell silent.

"I've got it!" cried Ariel, piecing the information together. "Mr. Kipper must be trying to make sure Mr. Chubb doesn't get the award!"

"Do you think so?" asked Coral. Her eyes widened.

"I'm sure of it," said Ariel, though she'd only just thought of the idea. "When he said *we* need to know what the class knows, he must have meant the award committee! And now he's trying to confuse us so it looks like we don't know anything at all!"

"But if that's true, what can we do?" asked Coral. "Ms. Finn didn't believe a word you said."

"I don't know exactly what we can do," said Ariel, "but somehow we've got to get to the bottom of this! Are you with me?" Ariel asked her friend.

"You bet!" cried Coral.

All afternoon Ariel watched Mr. Kipper carefully, taking notes on everything he said and did. When the bell rang at the end of the day, Ariel darted out of the class and motioned for Coral to join her in the hallway.

"What are we doing?" Coral asked.

"Shhh!" Ariel whispered. She nodded inside to Mr. Kipper, who was still at the teacher's desk, collecting his things.

"We're going to follow Mr. Kipper," Ariel mouthed.

Coral could barely hear her.

"What?" Coral asked.

"I said, we're going to follow Mr. Kipper," Ariel repeated, just loudly enough for Coral to hear.

"Follow him?" Coral gulped.

"Of course. That's what Mata Herring would do." Ariel opened up her book to show Coral. The third chapter was entitled "Mata Herring Tails Her Suspects."

"See, what Mata Herring did," Ariel explained to Coral, "was follow her suspects to find out what they were up to. That's how she got the goods on the general with the mustache. When she followed him, she discovered he was selling state secrets to the other side!"

"But why are we going to follow Mr. Kipper?" asked Coral.

"Because if he's up to no good, we'll find out."

"But where will we follow him to?" Coral replied in a worried tone.

"To wherever he goes, silly."

"I don't know about this," said Coral. "What if we get caught?"

"It's a free ocean," said Ariel. "We're allowed to swim anywhere we want. If he does happen to see us, who's to say we're not just out swimming around?"

"I *really* don't know about this," Coral repeated, shaking her head.

"Coral, listen," said Ariel. "Don't you want to find out where Mr. Chubb is, especially if he's in some danger?"

"Of course!"

"Don't you want to do anything you can to make sure that the best teacher in the whole wide ocean wins the Teacher of the Year award?"

"You know I do!"

"Well then," said Ariel, as if that were the end of the discussion.

"The only thing I'm thinking is—" Coral started to protest again, but Ariel clapped her hand over Coral's mouth.

"Shhh!" said Ariel. "Here he comes! Quick, let's hide!"

Ariel yanked Coral behind a row of lockers in the hallway. They stayed there until Mr. Kipper passed. When he was a fair distance ahead, Ariel grabbed Coral's arm and pulled her after her. The two mermaids followed their teacher, hugging the wall so they wouldn't be seen and moving as quietly as they could.

Suddenly Mr. Kipper stopped short. He turned and headed back toward the classroom. Ariel and Coral quickly ducked behind a trophy case. When Mr. Kipper reappeared, he was carrying a large, empty sack.

Ariel yanked Coral from their hiding place once again.

"This spying business is making me dizzy," Coral said.

"Shhh!" Ariel ordered.

Ariel and Coral followed Mr. Kipper out of the school, past the bustling shopping streets, and into a quiet residential neighborhood. Modest houses with colorful window boxes and flowering gardens lined the waterways. Neither of the two young mermaids had ever been to this community before.

The mermaids swam past a large square in the center of which stood a statue of a cloaked merman.

"Doesn't Mr. Chubb live in this neighborhood?" asked Coral.

"I think so," said Ariel. "I think I remember him telling the class about this square."

Ariel and Coral were swimming fast, trying to keep up with Mr. Kipper, who was swimming farther and farther ahead of them. Ariel kept turning her head around, this way and that, trying to see if she recognized anything else Mr. Chubb may have talked about—and she swam straight into a street sign.

"Ow!" Ariel cried out. She stopped to rub her forehead.

"Are you all right?" Coral asked. She waited for Ariel to catch up.

"I guess so," said Ariel. She looked around, trying to focus. "Oh no!" she wailed. "Where's Mr. Kipper?"

"I thought you were keeping an eye on him," said Coral.

Ariel sighed. "I guess we've lost him," she said. "Some spies we've turned out to be."

"Does that mean we can go home now? And get something to eat?" asked Coral.

Her stomach was gurgling from having skipped lunch to talk to Ms. Finn.

"No," said Ariel with determination. "It means we have to stay here until we find him!"

"I was afraid of that," said Coral with a sigh.

Ariel picked herself up and looked around. "He was going that way," she said, pointing down a street lined with houses. "If we swim in that direction, maybe we'll find him."

The mermaids swam down the narrow lane, with Ariel in the lead and Coral racing to catch up. The third house they passed had coquina-shell trim.

"Look!" gasped Coral, pointing to a mailbox. Painted on its side was the name "Phineas J. Chubb."

"It's Mr. Chubb's house!" said Ariel. "Come on!"

Ariel and Coral swam up to the large picture window and peeked in. Somebody was swimming around the living room gathering books and papers and stuffing them into a sack. It was Mr. Kipper! The two mermaids could see him plainly through the glass.

"What's he doing with Mr. Chubb's things?" asked Coral.

"What's he doing in Mr. Chubb's *house*?" asked Ariel.

The two mermaids watched, wide-eyed, as Mr. Kipper filled the sack and slung it over his shoulder. When he started to leave, they ducked out of sight.

"What do you think is going on?" Coral whispered to Ariel when Mr. Kipper was gone.

"It's obvious, isn't it?" Ariel said quickly. "He's kidnapped Mr. Chubb, hid him away somewhere, and now he's stealing things from his house!"

"Kidnapped?" cried Coral. "Stealing? But why?"

Ariel shook her head. "He must really be evil to go to all these lengths to make sure Mr. Chubb isn't elected Teacher of the Year."

"You think Mr. Kipper's kidnapped him just so he doesn't have competition for the award?"

"There's no other explanation," declared Ariel, convinced she was right.

"Maybe we ought to go back and tell Ms. Finn," Coral suggested.

"Not Ms. Finn," Ariel decided. "This time we tell my father!"

Ariel streaked through the late afternoon waters toward the palace. Coral swam quickly to keep up with her.

"What if your father's busy?" asked Coral nervously. She wasn't so sure about involving the King.

"I'm his daughter," said Ariel. "He can't be too busy for me."

Coral's heart raced as she struggled to swim faster. Ever since this day had first begun, Ariel had had her rushing from one place to another—to school, to the principal's office, to follow Mr. Kipper, and now to see the King!

Ariel swam up to her father's chambers of state. The door was closed. She reached to push it open.

"Don't you think we should knock first?" Coral suggested.

Ariel ignored her friend and swam right on in. Coral slipped self-consciously into the room behind her. At the far end of a long hall, King Triton sat on his throne. Sebastian, the royal court composer and the King's top adviser, was seated by his side. A group of lesser advisers was clustered around them.

"Ariel," said the King when he saw the two young mermaids. "What brings you here, my daughter?"

"I have to talk to you, Father," said Ariel.

"I'm afraid it will have to wait," said the King. "As you can see, I'm in conference."

"It really can't wait," said Ariel. "It's a matter of national security."

"National security?" said the King. He looked amused, but nonetheless he decided to dismiss all the advisers except Sebastian.

"Ladies and gentlemen," he said to them, "I'm going to have to ask you to take a short recess while I have a discussion with my daughter."

King Triton told Ariel and Coral to be seated. "So," he asked, "what information do you two young girls have?"

"It's about our teacher, Mr. Chubb," said Ariel.

"Your teacher?"

"Well, actually, it's about our substitute teacher, Mr. Kipper," Ariel chattered on. "Mr. Chubb's been out of school for a couple of days now with absolutely no explanation."

"You interrupted my cabinet meeting to tell me this?" the King asked, incredulous.

"Mr. Chubb is an important teacher," insisted Ariel. "He's the teacher from our district who's been nominated for the Teacher of the Year award!"

"Ariel, didn't you say this was a matter of national security?" Sebastian cut in.

"Well, maybe it's not national security *exactly*," said Ariel, "but it's a very serious matter. You see, Father, Mr. Kipper has kidnapped Mr. Chubb!"

The King put his hand to his forehead. He was trying not to be angry.

"No one will believe me," Ariel continued. "Not Ms. Finn, not Adella, no one. No one except my good friend Coral, of course." Coral smiled wanly and sank down in her chair.

"Why do you think one teacher would kidnap another?" asked the King.

"To foil his chances of getting the Teacher of the Year award!" Ariel said, as if it were obvious.

"Ariel," King Triton said with a sigh. "What proof do you have of this?"

"Proof!" said Ariel. "We've got enough proof to lock Kipper up for the rest of his life. First of all, he told us that he's got Mr. Chubb tied up!"

The King turned to Coral. "Is this true?" he asked.

"Sort of," Coral said weakly.

"All of a sudden, on Monday, for absolutely no reason," Ariel barreled on, "Mr. Chubb did not show up at school. Mr. Kipper appears in his place. Meanwhile, Mr. Kipper knows all about our class somehow.

Obviously, when he kidnapped Mr. Chubb, he forced him to tell him everything he'd need to know. And then when we followed him—," said Ariel.

"You *followed* him?" the King interrupted in disbelief.

"We certainly did," Ariel said proudly. "And do you know where he went? To Mr. Chubb's house! Then he proceeded to ransack the house and steal all Mr. Chubb's valuables. . . ."

"Ransack? Steal? Valuables?" The King looked to Coral for an explanation.

"Some books, some papers," Coral explained.

"Things that would be valuable to the Teacher of the Year," Ariel interrupted impatiently. "It's a good thing I've been reading this Mata Herring book about spying," she went on. "Otherwise, I might never have caught on so quickly, and I *never* would have thought to follow him."

The King leaned back in his chair. "So you've been reading about Mata Herring, have you?" he asked.

"I sure have," said Ariel. "She would have

had this situation taken care of one-two-three!"

The King closed his eyes. "Ariel," he said quietly and with great restraint. "I'm afraid my assessment of this situation is that your imagination has swum away with itself. Apparently this biography you're reading has gotten you caught up in the whole notion of spying. But from the evidence you've presented, I don't think it's likely that Mr. Kipper has kidnapped Mr. Chubb. I am sure, absolutely sure, that there is a reasonable explanation for everything you've told me."

"But . . . ," Ariel started to sputter.

"No buts," said the King, louder now. "You've interrupted an important meeting."

Ariel looked stunned as her father continued.

"This matter is now closed," he said. "I'm ordering you to leave Mr. Kipper alone. That means no more spying! I don't want to hear about either of you bothering the poor man ever again!"

"Yes, Father," said Ariel, lowering her head.

King Triton watched Ariel and Coral swim out of the room. "Sebastian," he said, "I want you to keep an eye on Ariel for me. Make sure she stays out of trouble."

"Yes, Your Majesty," Sebastian answered.

Outside the King's chambers, Ariel and Coral swam down a long corridor to the front entrance to the palace. They swam outside, heading toward the town, talking intently.

"Nobody believes me," Ariel said dejectedly. "And now no one is going to rescue Mr. Chubb."

"But maybe your father is right," said Coral. "Maybe there *is* a reasonable explanation for all of this."

"If anything has happened to Mr. Chubb, I'll just die," said Ariel.

As the two mermaids swam through town, they bumped into Mr. Kipper coming out of the freight office of the carriage station. He didn't seem to recognize the two mermaids.

"Excuse me," he mumbled distractedly, but didn't stop. As he swam past the mermaids, both Ariel and Coral saw that he was holding a book. It was one he had taken from Mr. Chubb's house!

"Reasonable explanation for *that*?" Ariel asked. "I don't think so. I've got to find out what he's been up to!"

"But your father told us we can't spy on Mr. Kipper anymore," Coral said.

Ariel thought for a moment. "I'll come up with a new plan," she said.

Coral shook her head. "I've had enough spying today to last me a lifetime," she said. "Whatever you're up to this time, count me out."

All the rest of the week, Ariel kept an eye on Mr. Kipper. Though her father had forbidden her to spy on him, each day she watched him carefully and added to the list she'd started. She couldn't get it out of her mind that she ought to *do* something. But she knew better than to act on her feelings. Her father would definitely not approve.

As the days passed, Ariel couldn't find out anything about Mr. Chubb. Each morning, at the start of class, Ariel would ask Mr.

Kipper when Mr. Chubb would return. Each morning, Mr. Kipper would shrug and change the subject.

One day after school, Ariel lay in her room, reading her Mata Herring book. "Coral may have deserted me," she said to herself, "but Mata Herring won't!" She paged through the book until she came to the chapter entitled "Mata Herring Tricks the Enemy."

Ariel began to read about how Mata Herring had often befriended enemies in order to get them to unsuspectingly confide their secrets to her.

"That would be a great plan," Ariel mused. "Except that *I'm* not allowed to do any spying." Ariel tossed the book down on her bed. "Wait a minute," she said to herself. "Father said he didn't want *me* to do any spying. He didn't say anything about anybody *else* doing the spying!"

Just then Ariel heard a knock on her door and looked up to see Attina, hovering in her doorway, looking bored. "Are you busy?" asked Attina.

"Oh, hi!" said Ariel. She made room on

her bed for her sister. "No, I'm not busy. Come in."

"You're still reading the Mata Herring book?" asked Attina.

"I sure am," said Ariel. "And not only that, I'm putting some of it to use."

"Really?" Attina's eyes widened. She sat down on Ariel's bed and listened as Ariel explained the whole long story. Ariel told her sister about Mr. Kipper and about spying on him.

"Wow!" said Attina when Ariel had finished.

"But no one believes me," said Ariel. "And now Father has forbidden me to do any more spying." She looked at Attina and smiled slyly at her sister. "So now I'm going to need someone to do the spying *for* me," she said. She paused, then asked, "Would you do it?"

"What would you need me to do?" asked Attina, a bit hesitantly.

"I need someone to ask Mr. Kipper a question for me, that's all."

"Hmm." Attina paused. "I don't know. I don't think I'm the best person for the task.

I think you need someone a little more outgoing. . . ."

"Maybe you're right," Ariel said as another idea popped into her head. "Maybe I need somebody who's *real* talkative. . . ."

"Adella!" both of the sisters said at once.

Ariel and Attina swam to Adella's room. They found her at her dressing table, polishing her nails while struggling with her math homework.

"Having trouble with your homework?" Ariel asked. "How'd you like some help?"

"How could *you* help?" sniffed Adella. "Your grade hasn't even studied equations yet."

"Not me, silly," Ariel answered. "Remember that new teacher of ours you saw swimming around school? He's super in math. I'm sure he'd help."

"*Your* teacher!" Adella protested. "I'm not even in his class."

"So?" said Ariel.

Adella looked suspiciously at her youngest sister. "What's the catch?" she asked. "There's something in this for you, I bet. What is it?"

45

"No catch," said Ariel. "All I want you to do is ask him a question for me. It's no big deal."

"Forget it. Ariel, I'm not getting involved in one of your crazy schemes."

"Adella," said Ariel, taking her sister's face in her hands. Flattery usually worked with Adella. "You are by far the prettiest of all the sisters."

"It's true!" Attina piped in, though both of them knew that all the princesses were pretty.

"You're the most charming," Ariel went on. "You're the best conversationalist with the most sparkling wit. . . ."

"I am?" asked Adella. She sat up taller in her chair.

"Well, you're *definitely* the prettiest," said Ariel. "Won't you help me?"

"What do you want me to ask him?" asked Adella.

"First you just chat a little. Ask him about your math, whatever," said Ariel. "Then when you've got him all friendly, all you do is ask, 'Where is Mr. Chubb, you scoundrel?' "

"Better leave off the 'you scoundrel' part," suggested Attina. "That'll just tip him off."

"It's almost dinnertime," said Adella. "Where am I going to find your teacher this time of day?"

"In the teachers lounge," said Ariel. By this time she knew Mr. Kipper's every move. "He goes there every afternoon after school and stays for hours. He doesn't seem to have anyplace else to go."

The three mermaid sisters swam out of the palace and toward the school. They peeked through the window of the teachers lounge and saw Mr. Kipper, just as Ariel had predicted.

Adella entered the building and knocked on the door of the lounge. Ariel and Attina stayed outside, hidden by the window so they could hear every word.

"Mr. Kipper?" Adella introduced herself. "I'm Adella, Ariel's sister. Ariel's told me what a super math teacher you are. I need some help, actually, so I thought I'd come by and see you."

Mr. Kipper invited Adella to sit down. He waited for her to continue, but Adella just sat there, staring at him, a blank smile frozen on her face.

"What's wrong with her?" Ariel whispered to Attina. "Talk to him!" she willed Adella.

But inside the teachers lounge, Adella didn't say a word.

"So," said Mr. Kipper after an uncomfortable pause. "You've come to ask for my help?"

"Yes," said Adella. "To ask you a question, actually. A question Ariel wants the answer to."

Ariel slapped her forehead. This wasn't what was supposed to happen. Adella was supposed to make small talk. And she certainly wasn't supposed to bring up Ariel's name.

"And what question is that?" asked Mr. Kipper.

"Where is Mr. Chubb, you scoundrel?" Adella asked slowly and carefully as if she were reading her lines from a script.

"Oh no!" gasped Ariel.

"Mr. Chubb?" Mr. Kipper looked as if he'd suddenly remembered something, then quickly glanced at his watch. "Oh, you've just reminded me. I need to get to the carriage station right away."

And with that, he bolted out of his seat and swam out of the teachers lounge and away.

Ariel and Attina emerged from their hiding places.

"How'd I do?" asked Adella when she rejoined her sisters.

"Terrible," Ariel told her and turned to Attina. "Come on!"

"Where are you two going?" Adella asked.

"We have to follow him!" said Ariel. She took off quickly with Attina in tow, leaving Adella blinking vacantly by the window of the teachers lounge.

"Where exactly are we going?" Attina asked while trying to keep up with her younger sister.

"We've got to get to the carriage station!" said Ariel.

"Why?" asked Attina.

"Because that's where Mr. Kipper is going. He may be trying to escape!"

"But the carriage station is in the other direction," Attina protested.

"I know that," said Ariel. "But the evening

carriage doesn't leave for another half an hour, so we've still got time."

"Time for what?" Attina asked. This was getting more and more confusing.

"To disguise ourselves," said Ariel. "Father mustn't catch us. If he finds out I'm following Mr. Kipper, I'll be in big trouble, and I mean BIG."

Ariel led her sister into the royal theater. They were about to go backstage to the costume room when a voice called out to them.

"Ariel! Attina!" It was Sebastian.

"Hi, Sebastian," said Ariel quickly. She knew they couldn't waste time talking to Sebastian. If they did, Mr. Kipper would escape on the evening carriage, and then she'd never be able to rescue Mr. Chubb.

"What are you two doing here?" Sebastian asked.

"We have to borrow some costumes," Ariel said without a moment's hesitation.

"Costumes?" asked Sebastian. He followed the mermaids backstage. "For what?"

Ariel was already in the costume room, rooting through one of the trunks. She

51

pulled out a flimsy veil and draped it in front of Attina's face, Mata Herring–style. "Attina, I think this will do fine," she murmured.

"Costumes?" Sebastian persisted. "Why do you need costumes? What are you two girls up to, besides no good?"

"Attina and I are taking dancing class," Ariel said. She nudged Attina. The two sisters exchanged a glance.

"That's right," said Attina, bobbing her head in agreement.

Ariel turned back to the trunk to look for more veils. "We'd love to stay and chat with you, Sebastian," she said. "But we're already late for class." Ariel draped two of the veils hurriedly over Attina and another couple over herself.

"I'm coming with you," said Sebastian, sensing trouble. "Your father's instructed me to keep an eye on you."

"I'm sorry, Sebastian," said Ariel. "But that's impossible. No visitors in class. Teacher's rule."

Ariel swam toward the stage door and motioned Attina to follow her. Time was running out. They had to get to the carriage station.

Sebastian didn't believe Ariel's story about a dance class one bit. He swam briskly toward the mermaids.

"I'm afraid your teacher will have to bend the rules just this one time," Sebastian said stubbornly.

Ariel stopped short. She knew she couldn't let Sebastian follow her to the carriage station. Not only would she be caught in a lie, but she knew Sebastian would tell her father what she was really up to, and that would mean trouble.

"Well . . . ," Ariel said, ideas racing through her head. "Well . . . if you're going to come with us, you at least need to be in costume, too." She headed back to the costume trunk, reached in, and pulled out a large, heavy turban. "Here," she said, slapping it on Sebastian and pulling it down so that it covered him entirely. "That fits you fine!"

"Ariel!" cried Sebastian.

Ariel grinned and nodded to Attina. The two sisters swam swiftly out the door and headed toward the carriage station while Sebastian struggled with the turban.

"Ariel!" he cried. "Attina!"

But by the time Sebastian finally wrestled his way out of the turban, Ariel and Attina were long gone.

8

When Ariel and Attina neared the carriage station, they could see Mr. Kipper waiting on the platform.

"Good!" said Ariel. "The carriage hasn't left yet!"

Ariel stopped to adjust her veils. "How do I look?" she asked her sister, and she spun around to show off her costume.

"Mata Herring couldn't do better," said Attina. "No one will ever recognize you. Not in a million years."

Ariel didn't know what she was going to say to Mr. Kipper. She only knew she had to stop him.

Mr. Kipper looked around and saw the two veiled mermaids swimming toward him. "Ariel, how are you?" he called out warmly, waving to her.

"He's recognized me!" Ariel said in horror.

Attina took Ariel's hand, and the two swam resolutely toward the platform.

"Ariel!" Mr. Kipper said brightly as the two sisters drew near. "What brings you to the station this evening?"

"Frankly," said Ariel, "you're the reason I've come."

"Isn't that nice?" Mr. Kipper chatted on. "You're my second royal visitor today. One of your sisters sought me out just a while earlier in the teachers lounge. Though I must say it was a rather strange conversation we had. If you could call it a conversation. . . . And who is it that you've brought with you now?"

Attina drew back her veil and extended her hand. "I'm Attina," she said, "another sister."

Mr. Kipper smiled broadly. "My *third* royal visitor!" he said. "I'm pleased to make your acquaintance."

"Mr. Kipper," Ariel cut him off briskly. "You and I both know why you're here, and I know that you know that I. . . . Well, I'm on to you!"

"On to me?" said Mr. Kipper. He shook his head in confusion.

"So you're going to deny it, are you?" Ariel went on. "You're going to deny that you're here to make your getaway?"

"Getaway?" said Mr. Kipper. "Ariel, what are you talking about?"

"Your getaway," Ariel persisted. "I don't know what you've done with our dear Mr. Chubb, but don't think you're going to get on that carriage and ride out of here scot-free. How low can you get, kidnapping one of the ocean's best teachers just so you can get your greedy little hands on that Teacher of the Year award."

"Let me get this straight," Mr. Kipper interrupted. "You're accusing me of *kidnapping* Mr. Chubb?" He stared at Ariel in disbelief.

Before Ariel could say anything further, the evening carriage pulled into the station.

"You won't escape!" cried Ariel. "Grab him!" Ariel called to Attina. "Quick!"

Ariel grabbed one of Mr. Kipper's arms, and Attina latched on to the other. The carriage pulled up to the platform, drawn by a proud team of sea horses. When the door swung open, out stepped none other than Mr. Chubb.

"Mr. Chubb!" gasped Ariel.

"Hello, Ariel," said Mr. Chubb. "Hello there, Kip." He threw his arm warmly around Mr. Kipper. "What a nice greeting committee."

Ariel and Attina let go of Mr. Kipper's arms.

Ariel looked from Mr. Kipper to Mr. Chubb, then back again. She didn't understand what was going on. But whatever it was, it didn't seem to be what she had been thinking at all.

Mr. Kipper looked directly at Ariel. "I'm here to meet Mr. Chubb and help him with his bags," he said.

"Meet Mr. Chubb? Help him?" Ariel

gulped. She turned to Mr. Chubb. "You mean Mr. Kipper didn't kidnap you?"

"Kidnap me?" Mr. Chubb laughed loud and hard. "Ariel, what exactly is going on here?"

Just then Sebastian swam up. He had Adella and Coral at his side.

"So, Ariel," Sebastian said. "Adella told me what you've been up to. She said you might have headed this way."

Ariel hung her head, growing more embarrassed with each passing moment.

"Your father's been alerted to the situation and has ordered you back to the palace, young lady," said Sebastian. "Now." Sebastian glanced around at the rest of the group assembled. "He wants all of you there, as a matter of fact."

"Me?" asked Mr. Kipper.

"But I just arrived," chimed in Mr. Chubb.

Both teachers looked nervous. Sebastian held firm.

"The King wants to see anyone who's been involved in, or in any way affected by, this whole crazy scheme."

9

When Ariel, Sebastian, and the others arrived at the palace, King Triton was waiting for them. Arms folded across his chest, he stared sternly at Ariel as she entered with her entourage. Ariel pulled off the veils, which were still draped over her head. She knew she was in trouble—BIG trouble.

"So, Ariel," said King Triton. "Would you like to explain to us all what's been going on?"

Ariel stared at the floor, too embarrassed

to look up. Her ears were burning, and she imagined her face was lobster red. She blinked back tears and tried to speak, but the words caught in her throat. She stared harder at the floor, wishing she could just fall through it.

"Well," said King Triton, "my daughter seems to have come down with laryngitis. Would anyone else like to explain what's been going on? Adella? Attina?"

Adella and Attina both stared down at the floor as well.

Finally Mr. Kipper came forward. "I think there's just been a slight misunderstanding," he said kindly. "No harm done, really."

"Something about a kidnapping, as I understand it," Mr. Chubb broke in. "Or a kidnapping that wasn't really a kidnapping. I just arrived, actually, so it's all a mystery to me."

"Mr. Chubb," said King Triton, turning to face the young teacher. "You've been away, is that right?"

"Yes, I have, Your Majesty," answered Mr. Chubb.

"And where exactly have you been?" The

King looked at Ariel to make sure she was listening to Mr. Chubb's response.

"Well, I was called away unexpectedly because of an illness in my family, Your Majesty. I had to leave rather suddenly. As it turned out, Kip . . . or rather, Mr. Kipper, here, was visiting me when I got the call. He and I are friends from way back. Mr. Kipper is a teacher as well, so I asked him if he'd take over my class for a few days. I briefed Kip about the class, sent a note to Ms. Finn introducing him, and was able to leave knowing that the class was in good hands."

"So you and Mr. Kipper are friends from way back, as you put it?" the King asked.

"Yes, Your Majesty. We went to school together."

King Triton turned and addressed Mr. Kipper.

"And Mr. Kipper," the King said, "you were on your vacation when you arrived here?" Again the King looked at Ariel.

"Yes. A sabbatical, actually."

"And it was out of the goodness of your heart that you agreed to take over Mr.

Chubb's class while he was attending to his family emergency?"

Mr. Kipper cleared his throat. "I guess you could put it that way," he said. "Just a favor for a friend."

"Mr. Kipper," the King continued, "after Mr. Chubb was called away, were you called upon to do any other favors for him?"

"Favors?" asked Mr. Kipper.

"Take care of anything in his house, that sort of thing?" asked King Triton.

"Well, he did notify me that he needed some things he had left behind—some books and papers—so I sent them to him by express carriage."

"That was very good of you," King Triton said.

"Just a favor for a friend," Mr. Kipper repeated modestly.

King Triton was now looking at Ariel directly. "Ariel," he said, "wouldn't you say it was awfully good of Mr. Kipper to take over his friend's class while his friend was attending to a family emergency?"

Ariel looked up at her father. "Yes, Father," she said weakly.

"What did you say, Ariel? I couldn't hear you."

"Yes, *Father*," Ariel said louder.

"Isn't it nice that the ocean is full of such generous-hearted people? I've always found that the people in my kingdom are more than willing to lend a helping hand to a person in need."

"Yes, Father."

"It's important to believe the best of people," King Triton went on. "Until it's proven otherwise. Ariel, I'm afraid that what has happened here is that you have jumped to quite an unreasonable conclusion based on a few facts you had at hand. You wanted to believe this whole ridiculous story that you created in your head."

Ariel could feel her whole face burning now. She wished her father would stop lecturing her, or at least that he would do it in private, not in front of a whole group of people.

"And the reason I tell you this in front of everyone here," King Triton said as if he were reading her mind, "is that I want you to take a look around this room at all the people you've involved in your scheme—two of your sisters, one of your classmates, and two of your teachers. If I'm not mistaken, you've involved your principal as well."

"It seemed like a good idea at the time," croaked Ariel. "It seemed like just the sort of thing Mata Herring might do."

"Mata Herring?" said Mr. Chubb. "Did this all get started because of that Mata Herring book?"

Ariel nodded her head.

Adella gave Ariel a look that said "I told you so!" Everyone else seemed to be staring at her, too, waiting for her to speak.

"So," King Triton said. "What do you have to say for yourself, young lady?"

Ariel looked slowly from one face to the other. "I guess I got a little carried away, didn't I?" she said sheepishly.

Mr. Kipper stifled a laugh.

"Is that all?" asked her father.

"No," said Ariel, her voice strong and clear.

"That's not all," she said. "I want to say I'm sorry. I really am. I'm *very* sorry. I

certainly didn't mean for all this to happen. I guess I was just worried about Mr. Chubb. I thought that Mr. Chubb might be in trouble. But I guess I went about things the wrong way. As you said, Father, I involved a lot of people, and I apologize to all of you. I hope you can all forgive me."

Even though he kept up his stern expression, King Triton was proud to see his youngest daughter handle herself so maturely.

"Well," he said, clearing his throat. "Thank you all for coming here. I'm sorry for any inconvenience this affair may have caused you.

"And Mr. Chubb," the King continued. "I hope the illness in your family is not too serious."

"Thankfully not, Your Majesty," said Mr. Chubb. "I was able to finally come back this evening because everything turned out fine."

"Well," said the King, "I'm expected at a diplomatic dinner, so you must all excuse me now. Sebastian will see you all out."

When the King left the room, Mr. Chubb and Mr. Kipper began to make their way to the door. Ariel swam up to catch them. She extended her hand to Mr. Kipper.

"I'm very, very sorry about everything," she said again.

"There's no need to keep saying that," he said, waving her words away. "You've already apologized."

"Friends?" asked Ariel.

Mr. Kipper took her hand and gave it a hearty shake.

"Friends," he agreed. "Ariel," he said, "though it's true you've caused a lot of trouble, I want to say that you've also proved yourself to be a very determined young girl, unafraid to pursue your beliefs."

"Not unlike many of our most important and most respected women throughout history," Mr. Chubb chimed in. "Actually, it's quite a testament to the book I assigned you. Apparently that book really captured your imagination."

"I couldn't put it down!" Ariel said fervently.

"Well, we always hope that our students will be caught up by the things they are reading."

"My sisters even said I'd caught book fever," Ariel continued.

"What do you think, Kip?" Mr. Chubb asked his friend. "Don't you think it would be an inspiration to the class, and to Ariel herself, if we asked her to give an oral report every month on a famous woman in history?"

"Great idea!" said Mr. Kipper.

"Would you like that, Ariel?" asked Mr. Chubb.

"You bet!" cried Ariel.

"Consider it a done deal," said Mr. Chubb, patting Ariel on the back.

"Wow!" Ariel said. "I hope you *both* get the Teacher of the Year award," she blurted out. Then she said good-bye to them both and swam off to join the others.

Sebastian had corralled Adella, Attina, and Coral and was taking them to task, repeating the lecture King Triton had just given.

The three mermaids were squirming uncomfortably, wishing they could be excused, when Ariel swam up to join them.

"So, Ariel," said Sebastian, ready to direct his lecture to her. "I suppose now you're ready to go back to being a princess and forgetting all the spy nonsense you read in that Mata Herring book?"

"Oh, I'm finished with that book," Ariel said. "And I've already got an idea for the one I want to read next."

"Next?" asked Sebastian.

"Yes. A biography of another famous woman, this one from the northernmost ocean. Joan of the Arctic."

"Oh, I've read about her," Attina joined in enthusiastically. "Wasn't she the peasant girl who led the king's troops in battle against the invaders?"

"Saddle the sea horses!" Ariel cried loudly. She charged playfully toward Sebastian, waving one arm as if she were brandishing a sword.

"Oh no!" wailed Sebastian. He toppled backward out of his chair and looked up at the young mermaid who was giggling and jumping about in front of him. He shook his head.

"Oh no," he said. "Here we go again!"